D0241611

For
Amber & Blake
Scout & Poppy

First published 2017 by
Mabecron Books Ltd
Briston Orchard,
St Mellion,
Saltash,
Cornwall,
PL12 6RQ

Illustrations Michael Foreman
Designed by Peter Bennett

Typeset in Garamond 3
Printed in Malaysia

ISBN 978 09955 0281 9

THE LITTLE SEA DRAGON'S WILD ADVENTURE

HELEN DUNMORE

ILLUSTRATED BY

MICHAEL FOREMAN

M

Mabecron Books

The little Sea Dragon did not want to go to the deep, dark, slimy wrecks to collect treasure with his friends and relations.

'All sea dragons love treasure,' said his father.

'What is treasure?' asked the little Sea Dragon.

'Gold and silver and rubies and diamonds,' said his mother.

'But what can you do with gold and silver and rubies and diamonds?' asked the little Sea Dragon.

'Don't be so silly,' said his mother. 'We always gather treasure from the deep dark wrecks. We bury it in slithery sea caves. That's what sea dragons have always done.'

'Boring,' said the little Sea Dragon. He wanted to go on a wild adventure. While everyone was polishing their scales to get ready for the journey, the little Sea Dragon slipped away to visit his friend Ailla. Ailla was a Mer girl.

‘I want to go on a wild adventure,’ said the little Sea Dragon.
‘I’ll come with you,’ said Ailla. ‘My mother won’t let me go swimming with the dolphins. She says I’m too young, but I’m not. I know where there is a strong current. We can ride the current so fast and so far that no-one will ever catch us.’

It was very early in the morning and the sun had not yet come up. The strong current wove its way like a rope through the deep dark sea. Ailla and the little Sea Dragon closed their eyes and counted to three. They plunged into the current.

It pulled them as hard as the moon pulls the tides. It pulled them as fast as a dolphin can swim or a whale can dive. Bubbles churned around their heads. Even when they opened their eyes they couldn't see where they were going. The current rushed and Ailla and the Sea Dragon held on tight to each other.

Suddenly the water cleared. Ahead of them was a cliff of sheer black rock. The current roiled and boiled and a huge wave reared up. It seized the little Sea Dragon and Ailla and hurled them high, high, high in a churn of foam.

It threw them down with a rush that tossed them over the rock and onto a wide white beach.

A second wave crashed over them and the little Sea Dragon and Ailla were buried in the sand. But they were still holding on tight to each other.

Soon they heard voices. Two children had come down to the beach before breakfast, to find the sandcastle they had built yesterday. But the big waves had come so high that there was no sandcastle left.
'It's gone,' said Blake.
'We can build another,' said Amber. 'Look at this! Someone has been making a sand sculpture!'

Amber walked around the shapes of the little Sea Dragon and Ailla.
The little Sea Dragon had sand in his throat. He wanted so much to cough, but he didn't dare.
'It's a mermaid,' said Amber.
'And a dragon,' said Blake, who knew about dragons.
'A sea dragon,' they both said.

The little Sea Dragon coughed. The sand quivered. Amber and Blake stared.
'Help us,' said a faint, faint voice. It was Ailla. 'Mer girls can't live in the Air.'
'It's a real mermaid,' said Amber.
'It's a real sea dragon,' said Blake.

They knelt down and started gently, gently pushing away the sand with their hands. Suddenly they heard barking. A man with a little dog was coming down the beach. The dog stood stiff and still, with its head pointing up. It barked and barked and barked. It knew about the Sea Dragon and the Mer girl.

'Nice sand sculpture!' shouted the man to Amber and Blake. 'You must have worked hard on that. Can I take a photo of it? SIT, Bramble, SIT!'
And Bramble sat on the sand, quivering with excitement.
The little Sea Dragon and Ailla lay still as still while the man walked around them, choosing where to take his photo.
'This is amazing,' he said. 'You kids have got talent.'

The camera clicked and clicked. The little Sea Dragon struggled not to cough. At last the man was finished, and he walked away with Bramble.

Quick, quick,' called out the Mer girl, 'I can't live in the Air.'
'What can we do?' asked Amber. 'The sea has thrown them right up the beach. The tide will never reach them.'
'We can't carry them,' said Blake. 'They're much too heavy.'

The little Sea Dragon heard this, and big tears fell from his sad eyes. He thought it was his fault. He had asked Ailla to come on a wild adventure, and now she was in terrible danger. If Ailla could not go back to the sea quickly, she would die. He cried and cried and his tears soaked the sand. Ailla felt the tears touch her seal-blue tail and she said, 'Cry some more, little Sea Dragon. Your salty tears are like the sea. They are keeping me alive.'

The Sea Dragon cried and cried and cried. At first his tears were a trickle and then they were a stream and then they were a river. Amber and Blake could not believe that anyone could cry so much.

'Quick, let's catch his tears in our buckets!'

Amber and Blake poured the Sea Dragon's tears over Ailla with their buckets.

Now she could breathe. Now she was growing strong. The salty tears loosened the sand around the little Sea Dragon and the Mer girl. The tears flowed and Ailla's beautiful seal-blue tail began to stir. She was moving. She was slithering and sliding towards the sea. Amber kept pouring the tears over her and Blake dug a channel as fast as he could, so that the tears would make a deep stream.

At last the Mer girl slipped into the shallows. She put her head under the water and breathed deeply as her hair floated around her like sea-weed. Behind Ailla the little Sea Dragon lolloped towards the water.

He was still crying, but he was smiling too. His scales glistened silver, as the sea touched them and washed away the sand.

'Sea Dragon, you are so beautiful,' said Amber, and she put her arms around him. 'I wish you could stay.'

Amber and Blake stood knee-deep in the water. Their shorts and t-shirts were wet with the Sea Dragon's tears. Ailla was in deep water now, plunging and diving through the waves.

'The sea is making her strong again,' said Blake.

Ailla lifted her head from the foam. She was smiling as she waved goodbye.

'She never even said thank you,' said Amber.

'Mer girls never say thank you,' explained the little Sea Dragon.

It was time for him to go. He wanted to stay and play with the children, but it was too dangerous. People would soon come to the beach and see him.

'You were very clever, little Sea Dragon,' said Blake. 'You freed the Mer girl.'

'Would you like my bracelet?' said Amber, and she took it off and hung it around one of the Sea Dragon's beautiful spines. The Sea Dragon tossed his head and the last of his tears flew away, sparkling in the sunshine. 'We sea dragons love going on wild adventures,' he said, and then he lolloped into the waves. Just before the water went over his head, he turned back to Amber and Blake. He thought they looked sad to see him go.

'Thank you!' he called, and then he dived down deep, deep, deep to find Ailla in the green and blue water. The little Sea Dragon and Ailla swam and swam and swam through the deep water, until they reached their homes.

When all the other sea dragons returned from finding treasure in the dark and slimy wrecks, they were cross with the little Sea Dragon.
'Where were you?' said his mother.
'You should have come with us,' said his father. 'You must learn to find treasure.'
'I did find treasure,' said the little Sea Dragon. He unwound Amber's bracelet from his beautiful spine and showed it to them.

All the sea dragons stared at the bracelet. They had never seen anything like it before.

'We must bury it in our treasure caves,' said the Sea Dragon's mother.

'No,' said the little Sea Dragon, 'I want to wear it for ever and ever.'

And the Sea Dragon did wear Amber's bracelet for ever and ever. But he never told the other sea dragons about his wild adventure.
Every time Amber and Blake go to the beach they look for the little Sea Dragon and Ailla, but so far they have never seen them again.
Maybe next summer ...